NORTH CAROLINA BASKETBALL

MARY-LANE KAMBERG

rosen publishing's
rosen central

New York

For Johanna Kamberg Falls #32

Published in 2014 by The Rosen Publishing Group, Inc.
29 East 21st Street, New York, NY 10010

Library of Congress Cataloging-in-Publication Data

Kamberg, Mary-Lane, 1948–
North Carolina basketball / Mary-Lane Kamberg. — 1st ed. — New York : Rosen, c2014
    p. cm. — (America's most winning teams)
Includes bibliographical references and index.
ISBN: 978-1-4488-9404-8 (Library Binding)
ISBN: 978-1-4488-9435-2 (Paperback)
ISBN: 978-1-4488-9444-4 (6-pack)
1. University of North Carolina at Chapel Hill—Basketball—History—Juvenile literature.
2. North Carolina Tar Heels (Basketball team)—History—Juvenile literature. 3. Football—History—Juvenile literature. I. Title.
GV885.43.U54 .K36 2014
796.323'6309756565

Manufactured in the United States of America

CPSIA Compliance Information: Batch #S13YA: For further information, contact Rosen Publishing, New York, New York, at 1-800-237-9932.

CONTENTS

INTRODUCTION

Some men's college basketball programs have winning seasons. The best of the best have winning traditions. Those teams include the University of North Carolina (UNC). The Tar Heels won the first varsity game they played. That was in 1911. Their winning ways continue today.

The team has won five National Collegiate Athletic Association (NCAA) tournament titles. It leads the nation with eighteen NCAA Final Four appearances. And, according to GoHeels.com, 154 Tar Heels have played in at least one Final Four game. No other school has had that many. The UNC Tar Heels play in the Atlantic Coast Conference (ACC). They have won seventeen ACC tournament championships.

Eight Tar Heels have been named national basketball players of the year. They have won at least one of six honors from the Associated Press, the National Association of Basketball Coaches, *Sporting News*, the John R. Wooden Award, the Oscar Robertson Trophy, and the Naismith College Player of the Year. Thirty-seven Carolina players have earned First Team All-American honors. And fourteen UNC players have won ACC Player of the Year, all according to GoHeels.com. Many Tar Heels have joined the National Basketball Association (NBA).

Tar Heels players excel in the classroom, too. Carolina players have won all-American academic honors nine times. And fifty-two players have made the all-ACC academic team, according to GoHeels.com.

The Dean Smith Center in Chapel Hill, North Carolina, has been home to some of the best college basketball players in the United States, including #35, Reggie Bullock.

Three hall of fame coaches have led the Tar Heels to glory. Frank McGuire served for nine seasons from 1952 to 1961. He left a young assistant in charge. Dean Smith was only thirty years old. At the time no one thought he would stay thirty-six years. After Smith left, Roy Williams took the job of head coach.

Together these players and coaches have made UNC one of America's most winning men's basketball teams. The team ranks third in the nation with 2,065 games won.

CHAPTER 1

WHAT IT MEANS TO BE A TAR HEEL

The University of North Carolina's 1910 football team was a loser. The squad had six losses and only three wins. Fans and athletes had months to wait for spring baseball. And nothing to cheer for.

Carolina officials hoped to ease the pain of defeat through the 1911 winter. They started a men's varsity basketball team. All they needed was a coach. And some players. The Tar Heels' track coach Nat Cartmell agreed to lead the team. And the school newspaper ran an ad for players. Twenty-five men showed up for the first practice.

The squad started its season against Virginia Christian. From the first game, the team played as a single unit. It never relied only on its stars. Before the game, team captain Marvin Ritch set the tone for the program. He said if one forward scored ten baskets and another scored two, it would count as six each. The same went for the other positions. He told the men, "Play for the team. Forget yourself." Carolina won the game 42–41. The team had a season record of seven wins and four losses.

A winning tradition began.

THE SOUTHERN CONFERENCE

Ten years later UNC helped start the Southern Conference. The Tar Heels played there for thirty-two years. In 1923–1924 the team went undefeated with twenty-six wins.

There was no national tournament then. The National Collegiate Athletics Association held its first tournament in 1939. But the 1924 team later got its due. The Helms Athletic Foundation formed in 1936 in Los Angeles. Its experts reviewed basketball history. They named national champions for each year from 1901 to 1939. UNC won the honor for 1924.

A live horned Dorset ram regularly joins Carolina football squads on the sidelines. On the basketball court, a caricature, known as Rameses (*shown here*), cheers for the Tar Heels.

Something else happened in 1924. Rameses joined cheerleaders on the sidelines. The live horned Dorset ram became the school mascot. A mascot is a symbol that brings good luck to a sports team. UNC's head cheerleader Vic Huggins got the idea from Jack Merritt, a well-praised fullback from previous years' football team. Merritt threw great blocks, so fans called him "the battering ram." Huggins proposed a ram as the mascot. School officials spent $25 to buy a live animal. They painted his horns blue and named him Rameses I.

THE ATLANTIC COAST CONFERENCE

UNC hired Frank McGuire as head coach in 1952. It was the last year Carolina played in the Southern Conference. In thirty-two seasons the Tar Heels went 304-111 in conference play. They won eight regular season titles and eight tournament titles. They had only three losing seasons.

Carolina joined the new Atlantic Coast Conference (ACC) in 1953. The Tar Heels went 21-21 in the first two seasons.

Frank McGuire took over as Carolina's head coach in 1952. Four seasons later he led the Tar Heels to the 1957 NCAA tournament championship.

They went 18-5 the third season. They shared the regular season title. But they lost in the ACC tournament. Only tournament winners were invited to the Big Dance.

The next season was perfect. The Tar Heels ended the regular season 24-0. They then won the ACC tournament, and they made the NCAA Final Four. It took a triple overtime, 74–70 win over Michigan State to make it to the championship final. In the final the Tar Heels needed another triple overtime. The Tar Heels beat Wilt Chamberlain and the Kansas Jayhawks 54–53. The team ended the year undefeated with thirty-two wins. The season was called McGuire's Miracle.

WHAT'S A TAR HEEL?

Tar Heel is a nickname for the state of North Carolina. It also refers to the people who live there. But it's best known as the nickname for athletes at UNC.

Where did the term come from? Different ideas exist. North Carolina is known for products that come from its pine forests. In colonial times the colony produced tar, pitch, and turpentine for the British navy. Pitch is a thick, sticky substance made from tar. The navy used it to waterproof its boats. Some say that workers who made the materials got tar on their heels.

Others say the term came from the Revolutionary War. Legend says that American patriots in North Carolina poured tar in the river between Rocky Mount and Battleboro. The gooey tar made it hard for enemy soldiers to cross. Troops that crossed the river said they got tar on their heels.

Another thought comes from the Civil War. In 1864 Major Joseph Engelhard wrote a letter about the way North Carolina troops held in battle. He quoted confederate General Robert E. Lee as saying, "There they stand as if they have tar on their heels."

The Tar Heels continued as a force in the ACC. Between 1957 and 2012 they won seventeen ACC tournament championships and were runners-up fourteen times.

MARCH MADNESS AND BEYOND

North Carolina stands out in NCAA tournament play. As of 2012, the Tar Heels have played in forty-three NCAA tournaments. They have a record of 108-41. And they have eighteen Final Four appearances—the most of any Division I school. UCLA is second with seventeen. Duke and Kentucky have fifteen appearances each. Kansas has fourteen. The Ohio State University has ten. Finally, Carolina has won the national championship five times—in 1957, 1982, 1993, 2005, and 2009.

Some Carolina players end their basketball careers at Chapel Hill. Others go on to play in the National Basketball Association. As of the 2013 season, 103 Tar Heels have played in the pros, according to Go-Heels.com.

As of 2012, the University of North Carolina Tar Heels had won five national championships, including the April 6, 1993, win over the University of Michigan 77–71.

CHARTER MEMBER TEAMS IN THE SOUTHERN AND ATLANTIC COAST CONFERENCES

The University of North Carolina helped start two sports conferences that still exist today. They were among the first members of the Southern Conference in 1921. They became part of the new Atlantic Coast Conference in 1953.

Southern Conference in 1921

- Alabama
- Alabama Polytechnic Institute (Auburn)
- Clemson
- Georgia
- Georgia School of Technology (Georgia Tech)
- Kentucky
- Maryland
- Mississippi A&M (Mississippi State)
- North Carolina
- North Carolina State
- Tennessee
- Virginia
- Virginia Polytechnic Institute (Virginia Tech)
- Washington & Lee

Atlantic Coast Conference in 1953

- Clemson
- Duke
- Maryland
- North Carolina
- North Carolina State
- South Carolina
- Virginia
- Wake Forest

As of 2012, forty-four UNC players have been taken in the first round of the NBA draft, according to GoHeels.com. That year, four Tar Heels were first round picks: Harrison Barnes, Kendall Marshall, John Henson, and Tyler Zeller. In the thirty-five years that ended in 2012, twenty-three NBA champion teams had at least one former North Carolina player on their rosters, according to BleacherReport.com.

A WINNING TRADITION

The Carolina Basketball Museum holds proof of the team's rich history. The interactive museum is located in the Ernie Williamson Athletics Center on the UNC campus.

The 8,000-square-foot (743-square-meter) facility cost $3.4 million. It contains photos, videos, and panels with statistics and history. Its collection includes the 1957 national championship game ball. It also displays an index card. The note on the card tells the coaching staff to "check out a kid named Mike Jordan."

Visitors will find Dean Smith's 1997 Sportsman of the Year trophy awarded by *Sports Illustrated* magazine. They will also get a glimpse of the present-day UNC locker room —a locker stocked with CDs, textbooks, and other items suggested by Tar Heel players.

CHAPTER 2

DECADES OF RIVALRIES

I t's game time. The players are pumped. The crowd is loud. It's easy to tell that this is an important matchup. The teams are more than mere opponents. They're rivals.

Rivalry exists when individuals or teams are evenly matched. And they want the same thing. Some rivals

Sportscasters nicknamed Interstate 40 "Tobacco Road," in honor of Erskine Caldwell's 1932 novel of the same name, to refer to the four basketball powerhouses along its route.

come from the same geographic area. Others are due to feuds between coaches or players. Most rivalries are simply intense competition. At worst they may result in violence both on and off the court.

Four rivals lie within 125 miles (201 km) of each other. The University of North Carolina, North Carolina State, Duke, and Wake Forest also lie 6 miles (10 km) or less from Interstate 40. The highway is often called Tobacco Road. The nickname came from a novel called *Tobacco Road* by Erskine Caldwell. It is set in Georgia. Its use in North Carolina refers to the state's tobacco crop. But sports writers use it most often to talk about the four basketball powerhouses.

The teams often face each other in championship play. For example, in 2005 three Tobacco Road schools were nationally ranked in the top five men's basketball teams, according to Alwyn Featherston, author of *Tobacco Road: Duke, Carolina, N.C. State, Wake Forest, and the History of the Most Intense Backyard Rivalries in Sports.*

NORTH CAROLINA STATE WOLFPACK

Between the 1940s and 1950s, North Carolina State University's Wolfpack were the alpha dogs of the Southern Conference. The Tar Heels were always the underdogs. At the time most teams—including UNC—relied on the set shot. But NC State used the one-hand push shot and fast-break to win games.

UNC hired Frank McGuire as head coach in 1952. He brought a new style of play. And the rivalry between the schools began. McGuire's first game between the two teams resulted in a 70–69 Tar Heel win. It also started a feud between McGuire and Everett Case, NC State's head coach. The two refused to shake hands on the court.

The rivalry came to blows in the 1954 ACC tournament game between the two teams. The Tar Heels pulled within one point of the Wolfpack in the last eleven seconds. After the score, Carolina guard Tony Radovich tackled NC State guard Davey Gotkin. In return, Gotkin beaned Radovich with the ball. Both benches cleared. The fight was on.

Between the 1960s and 1970s, Carolina dominated NC State. The Tar Heels won fourteen of fifteen games, according to Adam Lucas in *Carolina Basketball: A Century of Excellence.*

The rivalry between UNC and North Carolina State in the 1950s was so fierce, the two head coaches refused to shake hands on the court.

In the 1970s, NC State was back. David Thompson, a 6 foot 4 inch (1.93 meters) small forward led the Wolfpack. NC State beat UNC nine times between 1972 and 1975, again according to Lucas. The streak stayed alive until 1975. Phil Ford led the Tar Heels to break it 76–74. Carolina fans held up a banner that read, "The Streak Stops Here." And it did. Between 1975 and 2010, Lucas says, UNC won more than 73 percent of its games with NC State.

WAKE FOREST DEMON DEACONS

The 1950s saw a rivalry between Carolina and the Wake Forest Demon Deacons. For one thing, the two coaches didn't much like each other. And the squads didn't either. Before a 1955 freshman game at Wake Forest, the Carolina bus faced a barrage of hurled rocks.

Both teams had talent. Games were intense. In one game a brawl erupted on the court. Players on both sides blamed it on a fight during a football game earlier that fall.

Then there were what some called "cultural differences." Wake's players came from in-state high schools. UNC recruited talented but tough players from New York City. Many came from Catholic schools. In a 1956 game at Wake Forest, Wake fans held up a sign: "Welcome Brooklyn Catholics." The sign added fuel to the Wake-Carolina fire.

Despite the ill will, the Wake Forest team sent a good luck telegram to Carolina when the Tar Heels made the NCAA tournament semifinals in 1956.

SOUTH CAROLINA GAMECOCKS

In 1961, UNC coach McGuire moved on to the Philadelphia Warriors in the NBA. He stayed just one year. The team moved to San Francisco. McGuire stayed in the East. In 1964 he went back to the ACC—but not to the Tar Heels. Instead he became head coach for the South Carolina Gamecocks.

As before, McGuire recruited tough, physical players from New York City. In 1970 the Gamecocks had an undefeated season with twenty-five wins. The next year, the Tar Heels upset them 79–64 at UNC. The visitors turned their locker room into a disaster area. They tore doors off lockers. They broke mirrors and glass in a trophy case. McGuire's former athletics department billed him for the damage. He paid it.

VIRGINIA CAVALIERS

By the 1980s the University of Virginia became one of Carolina's main rivals. Early in the decade, center Ralph Sampson led a talented Virginia team. The Tar Heels had talent, too. Between 1980 and 1983, both teams were nationally ranked. They met in the 1981 NCAA Final Four. Carolina won 78–65. During the next two seasons, four of the five games between them had a spread of six points or less.

NCAA'S TOP TEN ALL-TIME WINNING TEAMS

UNC ranks third in the nation in overall wins as of the end of the 2011–2012 season.

1.	Kentucky	2090
2.	Kansas	2070
3.	North Carolina	2065
4.	Duke	1971
5.	Syracuse	1844
6.	Temple	1790
7.	St. John's	1737
8.	UCLA	1728
9.	Notre Dame	1723
10.	Pennsylvania	1697

DUKE BLUE DEVILS

Tickets for a Carolina game against Duke are always hard to get. A contest called "What would you do for Duke tickets?" is an annual event in Chapel Hill.

The Tar Heels and Blue Devils first met in 1920. At that time Duke was known as Trinity College. Carolina won 36–25. The modern rivalry is traced to the 1960s. Tar Heels guard Larry Brown had an ongoing feud with Duke forward Art Heyman. The two had been high school rivals. And both had verbally committed to Carolina. However, Heyman changed his mind and signed with Duke.

The Duke/Carolina rivalry was fueled by a personal issue between Tar Heels guard Larry Brown and Blue Devils forward Art Heyman that began in high school.

During their first game as college opponents, Heyman fouled Brown. Hard. Brown reacted. Soon players, coaches, and fans went at each other for ten minutes. Both players were suspended for the season. Brown later coached the Kansas Jayhawks to the 1988 NCAA tournament title.

As of 2012 UNC and Duke had not met in the NCAA tournament final. But they both made the Final Four in 1991. The Tar Heels lost the semifinal to Kansas, and Duke won the championship.

KENTUCKY WILDCATS

Two of the nation's all-time top men's teams share a proud record. Together Kentucky and Carolina have won thirteen national titles under five hall of fame coaches. They have two of the highest percentages of wins in history. Both schools helped found the Southern Conference in 1921. They don't play each other often enough to develop the kind of rivalry the Tar Heels have with Duke. But they often compete on the national stage. The teams vie for such major achievements as all-time wins, all-Americans, tournament appearances, number of weeks ranked number one, and even the number of times each appears on ESPN.

CHAPTER 3

AT THE HELM

In 1952 NC State was the team to beat in the Southern Conference. The team made it to the NCAA tournament. The first round game was set for its home court. The players thought they would win and advance. But they lost to the St. John's Redmen 60–49.

St. John's coach was Frank McGuire. He had served in Chapel Hill as a naval training officer. According to Adam Lucas in *Carolina Basketball: A Century of Excellence*, while McGuire was in town for the tournament, he said that "Chapel Hill was still in his blood."

Carolina officials must have heard him. The Tar Heels had ended the season in eleventh place in the Southern Conference. They wanted a new head coach. Why not get the guy whose club had clobbered the Southern Conference's best team?

NEW YORK CITY STYLE

UNC hired McGuire. His mission: return Tar Heel basketball to national standing. He accomplished that goal with an NCAA title in 1957. All of the winning starters came from the Big Apple.

The month before the tournament, *Sports Illustrated* ran an article. It called McGuire's recruiting style "basketball's underground railroad."

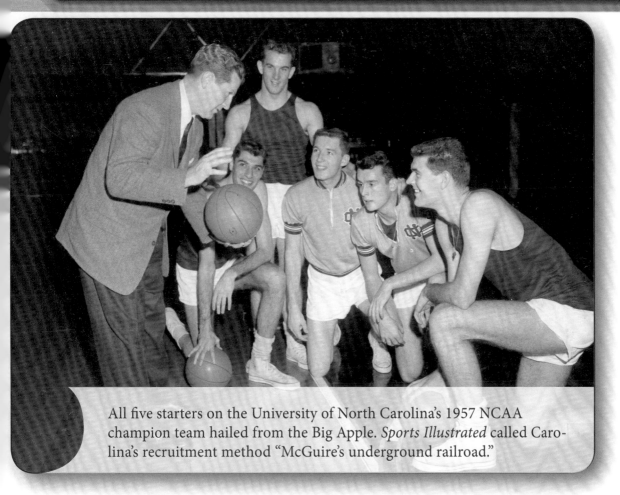

All five starters on the University of North Carolina's 1957 NCAA champion team hailed from the Big Apple. *Sports Illustrated* called Carolina's recruitment method "McGuire's underground railroad."

Soon the NCAA began an investigation. They thought Carolina spent too much on recruits and their families. They said costs of travel and meals in fine restaurants were excessive. The investigation lasted until December 1960. In January 1961, the NCAA placed the UNC program on probation for one year. The Tar Heels could not play in the ACC or NCAA postseason tournaments. McGuire was warned that he would not keep his job if any more rules were broken.

But a bigger scandal loomed. A Carolina player confessed to "point shaving." He took money from gamblers to hold back on scoring. He was not alone. The scandal involved twenty-nine players from twenty-seven schools in eighteen states.

McGuire left UNC in 1961. He had a 181-68 record over nine seasons. On his way out, he suggested his assistant Dean Smith for head coach.

THE CAROLINA WAY

Dean Smith grew up in Kansas. He played reserve guard on the Jayhawks basketball team. And he served as a graduate assistant coach under famed coach Phog Allen.

After the NCAA probation and the gambling mess at UNC, Smith took over the Tar Heels squad. School officials simply wanted a low-key program that followed the rules.

When Dean Smith took over as head coach, UNC wanted a program that followed the rules. No one expected his reign to last thirty-six seasons.

Smith brought stability to the program. He was strict but fair, his players said. McGuire let players "freelance" on offense. Smith brought set plays and set defenses. And he wanted his coaches and players to do everything the right way on the court, in the classroom, and in life.

Smith's coaching philosophy became known as the Carolina Way: Play Hard. Play Together. Play Smart. He also stressed the importance of everyone in the program—not just the superstars.

SEGREGATION IN THE SOUTH

Smith was a coach of the times. In the 1960s, many schools in the South were segregated. That meant people were separated according to race. In 1966 Smith recruited Charlie Scott. He was UNC's first African American scholarship athlete in any sport. Scott averaged 22.1 points and 7.1 rebounds per game. He earned all-American honors twice. He played on the 1968 U.S. Olympic team. And he played in the pros for a decade with such teams as the Celtics and Lakers.

Smith was not new to bringing races together. His father coached basketball at Emporia High School in Kansas. He added an African American player named Paul Terry to his roster in 1934. Emporia was the first integrated high school team in Kansas history.

Smith retired in 1997 after thirty-six seasons. He had 879 victories. His teams had twenty-seven straight seasons with at least twenty wins. His teams made it to the Final Four eleven times and won two national championships. He coached nine First-Team All-American players and thirteen Olympians. Many of his players left school early for the NBA. But 96 percent of his lettermen earned degrees.

FOUR CORNERS OFFENSE

In Dean Smith's second season at North Carolina, he introduced the team to a spread offense later called the Four Corners. One player—usually the point guard—stood on the free-throw line. The other four players stood in the corners of the offensive half of the floor. The Tar Heels used it to score "safe" shots. Or to stall the game.

Smith did not invent the Four Corners. Other coaches earlier used forms of it. One was Coach Spears, Smith's former boss at Air Force. Still, Smith perfected it. And he used it often.

The Four Corners won games. But it angered fans and opponents. In 1982 national television aired the ACC championship game between Carolina and Virginia. The Tar Heels won 47–45. They used the Four Corners to slow down the game for most of the last twelve minutes. A year later the ACC introduced the thirty-second shot clock to speed up play. After that the Four Corners offense lost its charm.

Bill Guthridge led the Tar Heels for the next three years. He retired in 2000. Officials offered Kansas coach Roy Williams the job. Sports media said Williams had a deal. However, he decided to stay with the Jayhawks. Instead, former UNC player Matt Doherty took the job. Three years later, UNC was again looking for a new head coach.

GOING HOME

Williams was still at the top of UNC's list. He had a 481-101 record in fifteen years at Kansas. And there were his North Carolina ties. He was born in North Carolina. Went to UNC. Played on the Tar Heel junior varsity. And he'd spent eleven years as one of Smith's assistant coaches. He was the one who got Michael Jordan to sign with Carolina.

This time Williams was in a different mood. Three years of conflict with KU's athletics director likely tipped the scale. Kansas fired the athletics director on April 9, 2003. But it was too late. UNC contacted Williams the same day. He packed for North Carolina.

In his first year as head coach, the Tar Heels posted a 19-11 season. They made it to the NCAA tournament. They lost in the second round. The 2004–2005 season was different. The Tar Heels lost their first regular season game. They won the next fourteen in a row. They won the ACC regular season title. And they were a number-one regional seed in the NCAA tournament. In the final game, they beat Illinois 75–70. It was Williams's first national championship as a head coach. Four years later in 2009 he won his second.

Roy Williams had too many ties to North Carolina to refuse the head coaching job at Chapel Hill the second time school officials offered it.

The next year he said, "Every single day, everything I do is based on one principle: how can I make Carolina basketball—the program, not an individual team—better today? That's how Coach Smith did it, that's how I do it, and that's how we'll do it together as we start these next 100 years."

Williams ended the 2012 season with a 257–68 record at Carolina.

And there is more to come.

CHAPTER 4

LEADING THE WAY

Forty-nine Tar Heel jerseys hang from the rafters of the Dean Dome. They honor the best Tar Heel players of all time. Eight of numbers have been retired. That means no Tar Heel will ever wear them again. Retired jerseys honor those who win one of the six National Player of the Year awards.

One belonged to Jack Cobb, a 6 foot 2 inch (1.88 m) forward. He played at UNC from 1923 to 1926. Cobb averaged fifteen points per game. He led UNC to the 1924, 1925, and 1926 Southern Conference titles. Cobb made the all-conference team all three years. Twenty years later, the Helms Foundation named

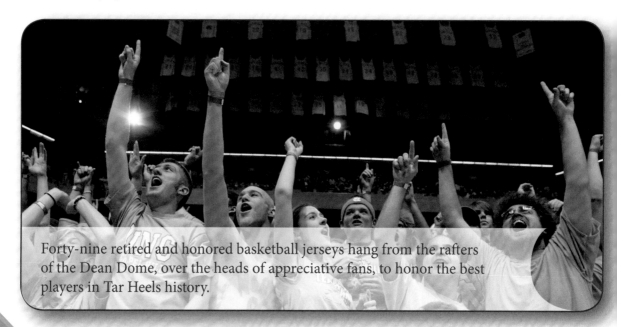

Forty-nine retired and honored basketball jerseys hang from the rafters of the Dean Dome, over the heads of appreciative fans, to honor the best players in Tar Heels history.

Cobb the 1926 National Player of the Year. In those days the shirts had no numbers. So a plain UNC jersey hangs in Cobb's honor.

THE BLIND BOMBER

He couldn't see well. But he could score. George Glamack, #20, played at UNC from 1938 to 1941. The 6 foot 6 inch (1.98 m) center wore thick eyeglasses. He could not see the hoop. To aim his hook shot, he looked at the black lines on the floor. He averaged 20.6 points per game his senior year. He set a Southern Conference record of forty-five points in one game against Clemson. Glamack led UNC to its first NCAA tournament. He was First-Team All-American. And the Helms Foundation later named him the National Player of the Year for 1940 and 1941.

FEED THE MONSTER

Lennie Rosenbluth, #10, could score from anywhere on the court. The 6 foot 5 inch (1.95 m) forward could make shots under the hoop. "Rosie" could also drop them from beyond what later became the three-point arc. He took hook shots, jump shots, and two-handed set shots. And he made most of them.

He was the heart of the Tar Heels' "Feed the Monster" offense. That meant "Get the ball to Rosie." In 1957 alone he scored 897 points—an average 28 points per game. His career rebound average was 10.4. As a senior, Rosenbluth was named the 1957 National Player of the Year, First Team All-American, and ACC Player of the Year.

"LITTLE PHIL"

With his father also named Phil, the son became "Little Phil" Ford, #12. Later he was called the best point guard in ACC history. He led Coach Smith's famous Four Corners offense. Ford was a slow runner. He couldn't dunk. But he was tough. He once lost a tooth during a game. He dribbled and picked up the tooth and kept on playing.

He was the first college player in history with two thousand career points and six hundred assists. His team record 2,290 career points held for thirty years. Ford was the 1978 National Player of the Year and First-Team All-American in 1976, 1977, and 1978. He won a gold medal in the 1976 Olympics.

As a junior, James Worthy, who wore jersey #52, led the Tar Heels to the 1982 national championship and won National Player of the Year recognition.

ONE-YEAR WONDER

James Worthy, #52, insisted on the best, from himself and from his teammates. He broke his ankle in his first year at Carolina. The ankle continued to bother him as a sophomore. But his junior year made up for it. For the entire 1981–1982 season, he and his team had their sights on the NCAA national championship. The goal was important to Worthy. The Tar Heels won the East Regional tournament. But Worthy made his teammates leave the nets on the hoops. Lucas in *Carolina Basketball* reported that Worthy told the players, "The nets we want are in New Orleans." They were on the way to the Final Four.

Worthy led the Tar Heels to the 1982 NCAA national championship. He scored twenty-eight points in the title game. He won honors as the National Player of the Year, First-Team All American, Most Valuable Player in the NCAA championship game, and the Most Outstanding Player in the tournament. He went pro with the NBA's Los Angeles Lakers the next year. In twelve seasons he made seven NBA all-star teams and won three national championships.

AIR JORDAN

A little-known freshman scored the winning basket in the 1982 NCAA title game. Mike Jordan, #23, made a 17-foot (5-meter) jump shot. And Carolina

Some freshman kid named Mike scored the winning basket for the 1982 NCAA championship. Who knew he would later be called the best basketball player ever?

beat the Georgetown Hoyas 63–62. In a YouTube video, Jordan later said, "That's the day my name went from Mike Jordan to Michael Jordan."

He still made jump shots. But he became better known for his "rock the baby" slam dunk. He was also known for his defense. During his three-year college career he averaged 17.7 points and 5.0 rebounds per game. He was the 1983 and 1984 NCAA National Player of the Year. He was also a First-Team All-American and ACC Player of the Year. He returned to UNC in 1986 to finish his degree.

In the NBA Jordan starred with the Chicago Bulls and Washington Wizards. He won four Most Valuable Player awards. He made the NBA all-star team fourteen times. He won two Olympic gold medals. And he is a Naismith Hall of Famer. Experts say he likely is the best basketball player ever.

DOUBLE TROUBLE

Forward Antawn Jamison, #33, averaged 22.2 points and 10.5 rebounds per game in 1998. He was the second Tar Heel to average a double-double for a season. (Mitch Kupchak was first in 1975–1976.)

Jamison had greatness thrust upon him. As a freshman in 1995–1996, he was to warm the bench behind Rasheed Wallace. But Wallace left for the NBA. Jamison had to step up. He did. He was the first freshman to lead the ACC. He had a 62.4 percent field goal percentage. He was also the first Tar Heel freshman to make the All-ACC team.

He played in two NCAA Final Fours. He won the 1998 Naismith Award. He made First-Team All-American and ACC Player of the Year.

HONORED JERSEYS

Forty-one jerseys hanging in the Dean Dome are "honored." They were worn by outstanding players who won at least one of the following awards:
- Most Valuable Player of a national championship team
- Olympic gold medal
- First- or Second-Team All-American
- ACC Player of the Year
- Most Outstanding Player in an NCAA championship tournament.

"PSYCHO T"

Center Tyler Hansbrough, #50, played forward from 2006 to 2009. In 2008 he won all six national player of the year awards. He is known for his hustle and energy. His nickname is "Psycho T."

On February 15, 2006, he set an ACC freshman record with forty points against Georgia Tech. He led Carolina in scoring and rebounding for each of his four seasons. And he holds the Carolina career scoring record with 2,872 points. He also made First-Team All-American and First-Team All-ACC four times.

Hansbrough could have left school early for the NBA. Others had left before him. But he wanted to earn a degree. And he wanted a national championship. His plan paid off. He earned a degree in communications. And he led the Tar Heels to victory in the 2009 NCAA tournament.

CHAPTER 5

GAMES TO REMEMBER

Acrowd of only two hundred watched Carolina's first men's basketball game. But they saw a winner. A century later the team still wins and more people are there to cheer. Every squad that hit the boards for Carolina likely played many memorable games. Here are some of the best.

Carolina has had plenty to cheer about over the years, including Frank McGuire's celebration of the 1957 NCAA national tournament championship. After his victory, he was carried off the court.

NATIONAL CHAMPS

The 1957 NCAA game between Carolina and the Kansas Jayhawks was one of the best championship finals ever. The Tar Heels were on a thirty-one-game winning streak. Kansas had Wilt Chamberlain, a 7 foot 1 inch

SIGNIFICANT GAMES

100th Win: At Duke, March 7, 1922
500th Win: Against NC State Wolfpack, February 22, 1945
1000th Win: Against Maryland Terrapins, January 29, 1972
1500th Win: Against NC State Wolfpack, February 7, 1991
2000th Win: Against Miami Hurricanes, March 2, 2010

(2.16 m) center nicknamed "Wilt the Stilt." He averaged 29.9 points and 18.3 rebounds per game. The Tar Heels had Lenny Rosenbluth.

The game was tied at the end of regulation play. But Rosenbluth had fouled out. Carolina held on through three overtimes. With six seconds left in the game, Joe Quigg sank two free throws. The Tar Heels won 54–53. It was a perfect ending to a 32-0 perfect season.

EIGHT POINTS IN SEVENTEEN SECONDS

It's safe to say that every game against Duke has been memorable. But the March 2, 1974, game stands out. It is known as the "Eight Points in Seventeen Seconds Game."

Duke was ahead 86–78 with seventeen seconds left in regulation. With time out, Tar Heel Bobby Jones hit both one-and-one free throws. Duke turned over the inbounds pass. And Carolina point guard John Kuester scored a layup. With six seconds left, the Tar Heels stole another Duke inbounds pass. Bobby Jones scored with an offensive rebound. The Tar Heels fouled Blue Devil Pete Kramer. He missed the first of a one-and-one. Ed Stahl grabbed the rebound and called time-out with three seconds to play. Walter Davis tied the game with a thirty-foot bank shot. Carolina won in overtime 96–92.

THE STREAK STOPS HERE

Carolina had lost its last nine games against NC State. The Wolfpack came to town for game ten on February 25, 1975. State's shooting guard/small forward David Thompson scored thirty-two points in the game. But it wasn't enough. Carolina led by eleven points at the half. Phil Ford scored nineteen points for the Tar Heels. And Carolina ran the Four Corners offense for almost eighteen minutes in the second half. As the game came down to the buzzer, bench player Mickey Bell nailed a free throw with twenty-nine seconds left. Carolina won 76–74. Tar Heels fans held up a banner that read, "The Streak Stops Here."

FANTASTIC FINISH

North Carolina was off to a terrible start in the fall of 1982. That spring Michael Jordan had made the winning shot in the NCAA championship final. But the Tar Heels lost the first two games of the new season. Their third game was against Tulane. It seemed headed for another loss. Carolina was down 53–51 with four seconds left. Michael Jordan got whistled for an offensive foul. But he stole the inbounds pass and shot the ball. He hit the 24-foot (7-meter) shot to tie the game. Carolina won in triple overtime 70–68.

THE DEAN DOME

The Dean E. Smith Center opened in 1986. It's fondly called the Dean Dome. The arena takes up 300,000 square feet (27,870 square meters) on 7.5 acres (3 hectares). It has four video screens for replays, stats, game highlights, and future game previews. It also has a standing-room-only student section near the Tar Heel bench. Warren Martin scored the first Tar Heel basket in the new arena. And North Carolina beat Duke 95–92.

COMEBACK KIDS

In the 1980s the Tar Heels and Virginia Cavaliers met nine times as ranked teams. The stretch included a Tar Heel win in the 1981 Final Four. On February 10, 1983, Virginia led by sixteen points at the half. With 4:12 left in the game, they still had a ten-point lead. The Tar Heels held on. James Braddock hit a three-pointer. Matt Doherty and Sam Perkins hit two free throws each. Michael Jordan pulled down an offensive rebound and scored. The Tar Heels were down by one point. At midcourt Jordan stole the ball from Virginia guard Rick Carlisle. Jordan took it to the hoop with a one-handed dunk shot. Carolina won 64–63.

On January 27, 1993, Carolina faced Florida State. The Seminoles were up by nineteen points with less than nine minutes left in the game. The Tar Heels went to work. They made a 28–4 run with tough defense and hot outside shooting. Carolina won 82–77.

The Sweet 16 game against Tennessee in the 2004 NCAA tournament saw the Tar Heels behind by seven points with five minutes left. Things looked bleak. Carolina's starting center Brendan Haywood had fouled out. That left point guard Ed Cota and two freshmen, Joseph Forte and Julius Peppers, to finish. The Tar Heels went on a 17–5 run to win 74–69.

TAR HEELS AT THE TOP

The Tar Heels fifth NCAA championship came on April 6, 2009. It was Roy Williams's second national title in his first four years as head coach. Carolina dominated the tournament. They were ahead for 230 minutes out of 240 during

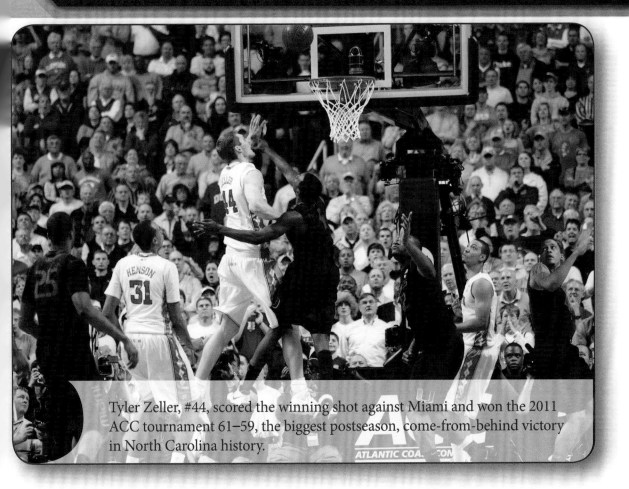

Tyler Zeller, #44, scored the winning shot against Miami and won the 2011 ACC tournament 61–59, the biggest postseason, come-from-behind victory in North Carolina history.

all of March Madness. They won all six tournament games by 12 points or more. Their average margin was 20.2 points. In the final game they beat Michigan State 89–72.

In 2011 Carolina was undefeated at home. They had won their fifth regular season title in seven years. And they were the top seed in the ACC tournament in Greensboro, North Carolina. The first round game against Miami was closer than they expected. In fact, the Tar Heels were behind until the last ten minutes. A 27–6 run brought them even with the Hurricanes. With 0.2 seconds left, center Tyler Zeller tipped in the ball. Carolina won 61–59. It was the biggest come-from-behind win in Carolina's postseason history.

1900 UNC includes basketball as an intramural sport.

1910 Carolina football team ends a frustrating 3-6 season.

1911 Carolina elevates basketball to varsity status. The Tar Heels beat Virginia Christian 42–21 in their very first game on January 27.

1921 North Carolina becomes one of the first teams to create the Southern Conference.

1924 The Tar Heels complete an undefeated season with a 26-0 record.

1939 The National Collegiate Athletic Association (NCAA) holds first national basketball tournament.

1941 North Carolina gets its first invitation to the NCAA tournament.

1952 Frank McGuire takes over as head coach.

1953 North Carolina helps found the Atlantic Coast Conference.

1957 The Tar Heels win their first NCAA championship. They beat Kansas 54–53 in triple overtime.

1961 Coach Frank McGuire leaves UNC to coach the NBA's Philadelphia Warriors. Dean Smith takes the reins.

1965 Carmichael Auditorium opens.

1982 Dean Smith wins his first national championship 63–62. Freshman guard "Mike" Jordan makes the winning shot with fifteen seconds left.

1986 Tar Heels defeat Duke 95–92 in the first game played in the new Dean E. Smith Center.

1993 UNC wins second national championship under Coach Dean Smith.

1997 Dean Smith retires. His former assistant coach Bill Guthridge takes over for three seasons.

2000 Bill Guthridge retires. Former Dean Smith assistant coach Roy Williams turns down offer for Guthridge's job. Former North Carolina player Matt Doherty takes his place.

2003 Matt Doherty leaves. Roy Williams, former Kansas Jay-hawks coach, becomes head coach.

2005 The Tar Heels win their fourth NCAA championship 75–70 over Illinois.

2009 The Tar Heels again win the NCAA tournament, defeating Michigan State 89–72.

2010 The walk-on team members adopt the name Blue Steel in practice and the media. They become known for sending tweets to Twitter fans from the bench during games.

2011 North Carolina opens the season October 12 ranked first place in both the Associated Press and the *USA Today* /ESPN polls.

2012 North Carolina ends the season with a loss to Kansas in the Elite Eight round of the NCAA tournament.

GLOSSARY

alpha dog The highest rank in a pack of wolves. A dog with a dominant personality and authority.

double-double A basketball statistic that means a player reached double digits in the same game in two of the following categories: points, assists, rebounds, blocks, or steals.

fast break A style of basketball play that quickly moves the ball from the defensive to offensive end of the court to try to score before the defense can establish position.

McGuire's Miracle The University of North Carolina's 1956–1957 undefeated season with thirty-two wins, including the NCAA tournament championship.

point shaving Taking money from gamblers to hold back on scoring, either to lose a game or to keep the score lower than expected.

push shot A basketball shot with one hand above the shoulder from a point relatively distant from the basket.

recruit To try to get an athlete to play on a team.

retired number A number that will never again be worn by a player for that team in honor of a star player who wore it.

rivalry A long-standing competition between two players or teams who are relatively evenly matched and who want the same objective.

scout To watch potential players or opponents to determine their strengths and weaknesses.

segregation Dividing people according to race for such services as restaurants, hotels, and drinking fountains.

set shot A basketball shot taken with both feet on the floor in a still position, often close to the basket. It is similar to a free throw shot, but it is seldom used in modern games.

Tar Heels The nickname of sports teams at the University of North Carolina.

Tobacco Road The nickname for Interstate 40, a reference to the state's tobacco crop as well as the nearby basketball powerhouses found along its route.

upset A win in a sports competition by a team that was expected to lose.

walk-ons Nonscholarship athletes who make the team.

Atlantic Coast Conference (ACC)

4512 Weybridge Lane

Greensboro, NC 27407

(336) 854-8787

Web site: http://www.theacc.com

This group of twelve colleges and universities meet for athletic competition. The conference includes the University of North Carolina, one of the founding members.

National Basketball Association (NBA)

645 Fifth Avenue

New York, NY 10022

Web site: http://www.nba.com

Founded in 1946, the NBA is a men's professional basketball league with thirty teams in the United States and Canada.

National Collegiate Athletic Association (NCCA)

700 West Washington Street

P.O. Box 6222

Indianapolis, IN 46206-6222

(317) 917-6222

Web site: http://www.ncaa.org

The NCAA governs twenty-three sports and more than four hundred thousand student athletes at more than one thousand member colleges and universities.

University of North Carolina (UNC)

210 Pittsboro Street

Chapel Hill, NC 27599

(919) 962-2211

Web site: http://unc.edu

Opened in 1795, the University of North Carolina was the first public university in the United States. In February 2012 *Kiplinger's Personal Finance* magazine ranked it first on its list of the one hundred best U.S. public colleges and universities.

USA Basketball

5465 Mark Dabling Boulevard

Colorado Springs, CO 80918-3842

(719) 590-4800

Web site: http://www.usabasketball.com

USA Basketball is the governing body for basketball in the United States. The nonprofit organization selects and trains America's men's and women's teams for such international tournaments as the International Basketball Federation World Championships and the Olympic Games.

WEB SITES

Due to the changing nature of Internet links, Rosen Publishing has developed an online list of Web sites related to the subject of this book. This site is updated regularly. Please use this link to access the list:

http://www.rosenlinks.com/AMWT/NCBB

Adamson, Thomas Kristian. *Basketball: The Math of the Game*. North Mankato, MN: Capstone Press, 2011.

Christopher, Matt, and Glenn Stout. *Michael Jordan* (Legends in Sports). New York, NY: Little, Brown and Company, 2008.

Johnson, Gary K. *Official NCAA Men's Basketball Records Book*. Chicago, IL: Triumph Books, 2008

Lacey, Theresa Jensen. *Amazing North Carolina: Fascinating Facts, Entertaining Tales, Bizarre Happenings, and Historical Oddities About the Tarheel State*. Lookout Mountain, TN: Jefferson Press, 2008.

LeBoutillier, Nate. *The Best of Everything Basketball Book* (Sports Illustrated Kids: the All-Time Best of Sports). North Mankato, MN: Capstone Press, 2011.

Lupica, Mike. *Long Shot*. New York, NY: Puffin, 2010.

Lupica, Mike. *Summer Ball*. New York, NY: Puffin, 2008.

Miller, Wes. *The Road to Blue Heaven*. New York, NY: Pegasus Books, 2007.

Monnig, Alex. *North Carolina Tar Heels* (Inside College Basketball). Minneapolis, MN: SportZONE, 2012.

Porterfield, Jason. *Basketball in the ACC*. New York, NY: Rosen Publishing, 2008.

Schaller, Bob, and David Harnish. *The Everything Kids' Basketball Book*. Avon, MA: Adams Media, 2009.

Slade, Suzanne. *Basketball: How It Works*. North Mankato, MN: Capstone Press, 2010.

Wilson, Paul F., and Tom P. Rippey III. *Tar Heelology Trivia Challenge: North Carolina Tar Heels Basketball*. Lewis Center, OH: Kick the Ball, 2010.

BIBLIOGRAPHY

Blythe, Will. *To Hate Like This Is to Be Happy Forever.* New York, NY: HarperCollins, 2006.

Brodess, Doug. "UNC Basketball: 12 Most Iconic Moments in Tar Heel Basketball History." *Sports Illustrated.* CNN.com, August 22, 2011. Retrieved July 4, 2012 (http://bleacherreport.com/articles/813288-unc-basketball-12-most-iconic-moments-in-tar-heel-basketball-history).

Chansky, Art. *Light Blue Reign.* New York, NY: Thomas Dunne Books, 2009.

Fowler, Scott. *What It Means to Be a Tar Heel.* Chicago, IL: Triumph Books, 2010.

Hoopedia. "North Carolina Tar Heels." Hoopedia.nba.com. 2011. Retrieved July 14, 2012 (http://hoopedia.nba.com/index.php?title=North_Carolina_Tar_Heels).

Lucas, Adam. *Carolina Basketball: A Century of Excellence.* Chapel Hill, NC: University of North Carolina Press, 2010.

Mills, Jeff. "2,000th Win Huge for Tar Heels at Home." *News-Record*, March 3, 2010. Retrieved July 5, 2012 (http://www.news-record.com/content/2010/03/03/article/2000th_win_huge_for_tar_heels_at_homeSPORTS).

O'Hara, Michael E. *The University of North Carolina Men's Basketball Games.* Jefferson, NC: McFarland & Company, 2008.

Puma, Mike. "He's the Dean of College Hoops." ESPN.com, March 13, 2006. Updated January 5, 2007. Retrieved July 9, 2012 (http://espn.go.com/espn/print?id=2366481&type=story).

Rutherford, Mike. "NCAA Basketball Rankings: North Carolina Runaway No. 1 In Preseason AP Top 25." SBNation, October 12, 2011. Retrieved July 23, 2012 (http://www.sbnation.com/ncaa-basketball/2011/10/28/2520883/ncaa

-college-basketball-rankings-ap-top-25-north-carolina -kentucky).

Smith, Dean. *The Carolina Way.* New York, NY: Penguin Press, 2004.

Walker, J. Samuel. *ACC Basketball.* Chapel Hill, NC: The University of North Carolina Press, 2011.

Williams, Roy. *Going Home Again.* Guilford, CT: The Lyons Press, 2004.

Williams, Roy. *Hard Work.* Chapel Hill, NC: Algonquin Books of Chapel Hill, 2009.

YouTube. "Down 8 Points with 17 Seconds." Retrieved July 8, 2012 (http://www.youtube.com/watch?v=oO445W4mtZI).

YouTube. "Michael Jordan Talks About Tar Heel North Carolina Basketball." Retrieved July 9, 2012 (http://www .youtube.com/watch?feature=endscreen&NR=1&v =uF532ghTvFM).

INDEX

ABOUT THE AUTHOR

Mary-Lane Kamberg cheers for the Kansas Jayhawks during March Madness. She specializes in nonfiction for young readers, having written sports articles for *Swimming World*, *Swimmer's Coach*, the *Kansas City Star*, and the *Kansas City Business Journal*. Her daughter played varsity basketball for the Olathe South High School Falcons.

PHOTO CREDITS

Cover, pp. 1, 7, 25 Peyton Williams/Getty Images; back cover (hoop) Mike Flippo/Shutterstock.com; p. 4 Streeter Lecka/Getty Images; p. 5 Grant Halverson/Getty Images; pp. 6, 13 (top), 20, 26 (top), 32 (top) 18 Lance King/Getty Images; p. 8 John G. Zimmerman/Sports Illustrated/Getty Images; pp. 10, 21, 26 © AP Images; p. 13 Terry Fincher /Hulton Archive/Getty Images; p. 15 Collegiate Images /Getty Images; p. 22 John D. Hanlon/Sports Illustrated/Getty Images; pp. 28, 32 Rich Clarkson/Sports Illustrated/Getty Images; p. 29 Jerry Watcher/Sports Imagery/Getty Images; p. 35 Cal Sport Media via AP Images; p. 37 Raleigh News & Observer/McClatchy-Tribune/Getty Images; multiple interior page borders and boxed text backgrounds (basketball) Mark Cinotti/Shutterstock.com; back cover and multiple interior pages background (abstract pattern) © iStockphoto.com /Che McPherson.

Designer: Nicole Russo; Editor: Bethany Bryan;
Photo researcher: Karen Huang